ALL MOONS ARE NOT ALIKE

Heart Tales of Two Lands

BY

Richard Alberto Morillo Guevara-Fabra'

Andrea T. Goldreyer, Editor

James A. Morillo
Co-editor

Cover Illustration
"Come in me, take me away, shadow of the moon May 2018.
By Carlo Salomoni Pittori/Illustratore/Scultore/Progettista
Carlosalomoni@gmail.com   Mobile 053256188
Ferrara, Italia.

PUBLISHED by SOUTHERN MOUNTAINS PUBLISHING Ltd.
Merrick, New York. USA

southernmountainspublishing@gmail.com

Library of Congress Cataloguing-In Publishing Control Number 2019900873

ISBN 978-0-9863863-4-3

United States of America Copyright.

2018

First original edition.
February 2019.

*Lovingly dedicated to all Poetry readers around the world,
especially for those who allow a collective of words
become images, emotions and a catalyst that
ignites the light in their heart and soul!*

ALL MOONS ARE NOT ALIKE

Heart Tales of Two Lands

ALL MOONS ARE NOT ALIKE – Heart Tales of Two Lands.
Table of Contents

LET'S

From the banks of launched inherited winds, the sediment of my soul is
spitting sterile prayers beyond the saltwater cliffs into the atmosphere.

Let the alluring cries gleam as we endure in the convenient vortex that
limits our allotted poison without any remorse.

We are endowed by the conceived streams glossing over the light
of darkened water in complete disarray.

Let's transform eternity into a departing haunting dirge that murmurs
with solemnity by setting the blizzard of snow on fire.

Let's pluck the dimpled breaths of the evening air emboldened by our
spirit that still is very much alive.
The light is visiting us all dressed in bold colors.

Let's unsheathe all darkness and riddle it with strands of liquid light,
so we may be able to dialogue with the stars before they fade in
the flash of the day that flows out___ craving rivers of
silence and ancient _____ emptiness!

Let's brace to rest on the revealed footprints pulled in by closing
time. Let's shrug the dawn of sunset, as we harvest our history.

December 20, 2018.

THE DAWN IN SPRING

Lurking behind the mist of daybreak, your perfume rides on
fatigued shrouded gray clouds behind three masted fog.
You can hear lyrical ballads, hymns and chants that map
the quiet thunder during these invented spring times
that awaken the soil.

I once embraced the stars that hid in the corners of the
heavens only to see them later spread out in the rest
of the sky before they sprung like pensive
witnesses on a stained night.

Daybreak light shone coming out of a slit in the azure
falling away from some jasmine magic carpet that
was riding on the skirts of clouds.

They surged on sail boat shaped veils carrying sea
sketches in their hearts along with our names
carved in misty fog.

Dawns in spring are to be found in islands of nests filled
with woven songs and hymns sung to the dawn's lost
tides. They are carried by unknown oarsmen rowing
away with our ephemeral light toward far away cliffs.

Our leftover glow is mystically shackled to the glaze of
the shadows of my words which walk hand in hand
with those of my poem in the early light of dawn.

The dawn of spring carries drops of formless gleaming
silence in the halls of peace, as I quietly crawl
upon an empty molecular waning sunrise!

We've just begun a new day.

September 22, 2012.

DARE

Dare to listen to the handcrafted moon's voice that challenges the
morning shorelines on uncharted fields.

Dare to gaze at the remnants of rivers waning in circuits of
unidentified lands whispering uneasy untested storms.

Dare to catch a drifting rainbow napping in weaving lonesome
landscapes that vanish inside shadows of wasted moist dust.

Shoplift the tender views of the moon and its brood burning
candles at seaside's unknown lands illuminating your path.

Dare to explore and soar above fading lights for roaming lost
souls narrating beleaguered, meandering self tales.

Dare to paddle and row away from expectant waves that bring
sorrows and tears from un-expected covering clouds.

Don't be afraid to divert the exploding twilight as well as
to subvert your burning dreams.

Don't let despondent Earth breathing grime and debris be
your final destination.

Dare to capture the fledgling lights which ride on rails of
brightening skies toward your destiny.

Spit and glare down at your vacant bones and requiem sounds
of church bells that admonish you that it is too late to dare.

June 02, 1991.

THE MIDNIGHT TIDE

As I laid fading in the crawl of the night, I found myself skimming
over the land of the vast sea.

The weather slowed to slowest. I had no time to blurt out your name
in the middle of my long desperate road.

The serene night that was on a lease became fleeting and elusive
as it loosened itself from the piers to which it was
assigned, and fled.

There was no time to plead or even howl as I seemed to be
wrestling with the ever unwinding twilight of tapestries
which the darkness brought.

My last night was just beginning when your face came galloping
along, submerging itself in this most drinkable of nights, to
remind me that I must not become a prisoner and a refugee
of despair nor of the music of the lyre.

You reminded me that I must not succumb to the swagger of the
night, as the midnight tide was haunted and its grin was
just temporary.

It will recede as soon as the moon motion cycle hides behind
its apogee and my moist disobedient feeble corneas.

The skeletons of the morning are showing their face, along with
the voice through the swells of the sun's eyes.
The midnight tide is approaching.

August 22, 2015.

THE RIDGE OF THE NIGHT

*As the night disrobes before me, its serenity is disturbed by your
sinful figure reflected in my darkened mirror that
breathes passion.*

*It crosses borders that leap over walls and zones with arms
that spill desire with white fangs under a moonless sky.*

*After hiding in the bark of the shadows, you leapt over
glimmering alluring gardens to crouch in my abode of
rose petals and bruised idle cells that were overrun
by the flood of fire in the night.*

*The silhouettes stalked each other until they finally subdued
one another into an amorous submission by screaming
veins overflowing.*

*We were like two extinct animals in the fauna foraging and
forging an oasis of dreams next to rivers in need of rest
until the first blush winked its sweet blaring whimper.*

Evolution was continued!

September 13, 2003.

WILLING TO DISCOVER

I surf close to the mangroves and dive among the reed sweet-grasses as I explore the new shores attempting to reconstruct our first touch on dry land.

I challenge myself to discover the grooves of the wormholes and meteors through which I will teleport myself to travel the uncharted and yet undiscovered Cosmos.

August 12. 2011.

IN ALCOVES OF SILENCE

*A lukewarm murmur welcomes me accompanied
by a bouquet of caresses, which until today had
remained bottled in alcoves of silence, walled
by rivers woven and quilted in silver by the
eventful history and its rugged Orography.*

*Between fragments of forgotten petals, the
inseparable hearts accompany me to the
flesh of a new destination, to an original
landscape of reality, more to the smile
and the twinkles of love.
To the profane thresholds that wallow
in the garden of shadows.*

*I walk the omitted furrows where the passions
of love spills in desired, designed and painted
abstract glaciers dancing over borders
that melt on the lines of my youth.*

*Love and loneliness is the mythology;
symbol of lies, desires and myths.*

*I wash my face with the darkness, and withdraw
my name and image from the obituary notice.*

*I would love to inherit the earth before they cry
for my absence.*

December 31, 2012.

SONG IN OCTOBER

Its musical content plows my mind;
Straddling, grazing my framed land
that exposes my bone marrow...

Autumn sounds bounce and blur while mixing
with the rumors that travel as an invasion of
notes hiding behind the docile masks of the
people of "mi barrio".
It's Carnival time!

In defiance of the danger of the streets, the
crying tone of my song in October hovers
over forests of people spilling from
the sidewalk, drunk from dancing.

As maternal voices dart across the air asking
for succor, they gasp rapturous enchants
that light our history.

Our songs in October carry notes that are
antagonistic and haunting all at the
same time; lamenting my absence
through its pores in dances and
fiestas in the streets of 'mi barrio'.

June 01, 2002.

RECLUSIVE SUNRISE

I saw the next reclusive sunrise whisper a rhapsody
in a dialect that only your heart could comprehend.

It wanted to curl in your heart. It wanted to craft exalted
hymns to the joyous remembrances and the profound
love that once bloomed in your atrial
affectionate residence.

You know I was the bricklayer that once built a love
palace to our dreams.

Now I'm perched on the left side of the moon endeavoring
to resurrect and cradle our charred voices so we
can sing together once more.

There's still time to sing a duet of allusive songs. I swear
to you, they will not be sung acapella, for the humming
of the moon's distant roar will be accompanying us.

Let's find a roundabout in the sky. Let's peel the layers
of frozen rubble behind from which you hide
the remnants of our love.

Let's borrow the book of hope from my dream shelf before
it fades and degrades. Let's wag the tail of time.

Don't skip and jump over my illusion.
Let's retrace our dreams.
Let's go inside a time capsule full of history,
ardor and peace.

Please let's go on!

January 09, 1998 – October 23, 2014.

WHEN AWAKENING AT DUSK

*Should we defend the land? Should we rudely, suddenly understand that
the once ephemeral is now just that...When do we become acquainted with
the full knowledge that the familiar is fading in between the shadows
of the years, as they go by riding on waves of foam towards infinity?*

*When is it time to stop visiting the harbors for fear of being forced
to be escorted onto ships heading to apocryphal lands?*

*When does our ship join the convoy to ride inside darken storms
without having any definitive short term destination or long
term coastal pawned shelters?*

*When does the illusion that we can separate ourselves from our own
flesh while we are still alive takes place? When does the infinite
light begin to dissipate, before our mind and eyes not notice it?*

*Why can't we wake up at the dawn of our life, as opposed to
opening our eyes to barely notice the dusk of our years?*

*Why can't we include the Septuagint as part of our epistles in our
fluttering life filled with far flung earthly hunger for knowledge?*

*Years of pain and song less bird sounds live inside my inner solitude
without hearing the elementary voice of the earth. I still do hear the
rattle of the ghosts of my watered down dreams riding in the dust
of faceless stars in my head.*

*Waterfall running water fills my garden night, even as the flowers
of spring are careening towards swindled winters.*

*Am I looking to go back to the womb? Where the pit fire amber
mistresses will warm my soul in an innocent but noble
anarchic ceremony to cleanse and spice my spirit?*

August 22, 2004

MORNING MOON

*Behind the window pane to the sky, we are establishing our
presence in between mountains of clouds, before the
night leaves its slumber to give birth to the dawn
of the peaceful light.*

*We are thrusting ourselves past processions of visions leading
us beyond beds of levitating stars moving upstream past
our interrupted morning moon.*

*The heavens are cloaking its secrets under un-named meteors
and planets' brushstrokes, on our way to the promise land
being unfurled before us.*

*The azure is painting swarms of colors with the drifting light
encircled by archipelagos of fire and dust hovering above
storms and thunder behind drawn curtains.*

*I'm wearing the greeting light of a blue aurora arriving on a
floating dugout canoe. Its incoming rays are brightening
my darkened lapel.*

*We are crawling out from under a garden of stars conversing
away yesterday's laments.*

Hello morning moon!

November 28, 1998.

AT THE PORCH OF AN IMAGINED CENTURY

The stroke of midnight sound rose as a mushroom cloud, as tulips
saluted the sun to discover their liliaceae.

My years are being sponged in the midst of the gathering pain in
my bones, mapping and etching on the stem of the earth.

The years ring in the hours and days of our heedless history before they
plummet away. Now they are attempting to harvest
light from darkness.

The moon advances a heedless proclamation roaring past the wrinkled
tumult at the kiln burning silence _at the gate of my imagined century.

The remaining light hums away from the veranda, leaving its mark as
sentinels riding on the rail of volcanic shadows.

From the steps of the portico, the metal framework's sound grazes the
stars, unleashing a multitude of strands reaping the lost years.

Crowded armies of shadows are weeping before genuflecting at the
porch before the dew. The carracks are sailing trampling across
blind seas' borders.

The echoes of centuries are concealed by the haze yarning the shade
of droplets of silence. They are as sleeping voices pulsating past
drenched mountains with age.

The vanishing hours are scheming to dream and sing along the seasons
visiting drunken creeks and empty buried plots harnessing
smuggled yearnings.

Unleavened coveted waterfalls in the sky are flying as air gondolas
once held captive by primitive wounded rivers floating
on still-born vacant fluyts.
May 31, 2012.

12

SILENT CORRESPONDENCE

With resounding joy, I am swept by the transformative vision of
your landscape, as its sloping coastline invades my province's
sky with its earthly gifts.

With selected intention, I pluck a feather from your embroidered light,
so the sun won't drown me at the outbreak of my promising journey.

Through different constellations, I travel in search of clear signals in
your scintillating eyes as well as from your flaunting frame, all
the way to the sway of your invasive wind-up.

At dusk, a river of unhindered silence bathes me in its waters. With
this action, you are sending me laconic correspondence adhering
to my contemplative craving heart.

The blue pain of my bones, are the lookouts at the edge of my dreams
conversing inside the brothels of our reality while you ignore
my self-evident manifesto.

How do I decode the quiet dreams living in your sacred and mysterious
nest, as well as your storied infinite smile that hoists my
spirit beyond a hush?

I watch the flowering of the night hours prevail before me, prior to the
morning's ailing movement, its unknown geography fading
into an unkind sepulcher.

Streamlined lights fade on to a grieving wound close to the beginning
of my fable which has you as its hero moving past the
tyrant wolves of our identified truth.

Is this an absurdist's yearning doomed to failure? Please bestow hope
so I may dream about walking out with a smile, after dissolving
into each other, awakening the dormant energy that will
defeat my tyranny of despair.
March 30, 2012.

FROM THE GLEN

Out of the depths of a fractured fantasy, Eugenio and I arose full
of brio past forbidden waters and usual stench.

From this ravine carved by the "Machangara" in the outskirts of the city,
we surged as the thorn and the flower, always together full of audacious
life and flight in the already tired doleful afternoons after school.

With indefinable impulses, we skipped and jumped past Flora that covered
over ninety percent of the inclining landscape on our way to explore
the cavernous waterways and the monuments of boulders
that decorated this ancient land.

Cheering our fate past the turmoil, we stood as indefinable sovereigns
that ruled the land of the clouds and despair where the Flora and
Fauna spread its wings to agitate the soil to message us that
our soul belonged here.

Over the empire of sweeping cauldrons of clairvoyant winds, we
declared ourselves to be eager forerunners of a history that
enveloped our credulous spirit as we traveled alee on
the back of an insatiable will.

From the arroyo that cut across the old historical canyons of the Incas,
we faced the Daedalean task to bifurcating terrain on our very
young feet with the verve and tenacity that only our foolish
youth could provide.
This excursion into the known, and yet prodigiously obscure roar of the
naked unpredictable road, quenched our thirst to fill the hours with
the hums of history and discovery filling us with immense joy.

On the road, we found that within the notes of the verses of birds
and the gurgling sounds of the streams, the value of reliance on
friendship, love, and support on one another was discovered.
It was in these allied trails and drifting skies where we buried our
bereaved songs and learned to dialogue with ourselves!
May 01, 1985.

I'M STILL IN TRANSIT

I pilgrimage through layered landscapes where
my tears stampede entwined behind the
honeycomb of limbs drifting close to
another life's dream catcher.

I'm still in transit past the parade of mythology
preying upon my forfeited confinement, still
binding me to the scaffolding of
this disarrayed Earth.

June 01, 1982 – May 31, 1992.

NOCTURNAL FURNACES

Starving nights followed hurried flocks of moonlights
under which a rustle of voices are drifting
to accompany me.

Stillbirth winds are resting on our splattered
forsaken setting awash in colors on
top of unshaven grasses.

Nocturnal furnaces warm the word museum
being created by threading an elaborate
quilt geared up for the fire.

October 09, 2008.

ALMOST SILENCE

River water carves out the granite ravine
as roaring silence is interrupted
by my hoarse imprisoned echo
traveling in your direction.

Its stream carries my departed voice
of anguish. It is trying to put back the
pieces of lost memories between
the face of agile currents looking
for its origins.

The capillaries of silence are flowing away
from its nocturnal and semi-diurnal
hemispheres aligned with the moon.

There is still time to explore life's silent
ship before mourning.

It's another day for the absence of light
and cydic music to be recorded only
in the core of our soul, while we
exhume the reverberation of
sounds' birth in Poetry.

The fate of crowded silence is being
determined; it is perishing by
crashing amid the clatter of
rain on fire...
before barking and spitting life
as it scatters unceremoniously!

June 01, 2018.

EVEN THE FALLEN CAN STILL LOVE

Praise the moon as it shimmers in total darkness.
The withered stone still guards the weak,
and the fallen. It dauntlessly loves torn
noble hearts that go on past nightfall.

The splendor of the fallen... bleeding, still crave
to love their mother, children, fellow man
and their land. Despair doesn't rest. On its
knees it still glows with the star's splendor.

Moaning our sorrows is the ancient art of dusting
one's underlying grief, so as to be able to continue
to love, radiate compassion as well as rein-in
interwoven midnights.

Compassion is to be had even by the fallen that
can still love, and continue to live,
eavesdrop on hunger while they
nibble with the self-sufficient and their heirs.

Can we still run errands for the dead
who loon their moans for the living?

October 20, 2017.

18

I WON'T DANCE ON YOUR TOMB

*The rich dark baseboards on my porch are the same as those in a
revolving door, part evidence for they who believe in the
convoluted tradition of the origins of re-incarnation.*

*I don't wish to hear the chants with apostolic fervor that
call us to loath the vanished and hold them in contempt,
for they are still troubadours in my life.*

*Soon I might be one of the wretched having intercourse with
the gods of the fallen, speaking in lost languages in
sorely missed sunken swamp islands.*

*Beyond the smoking rivers of mist, the birds sip the top of
the foam swimming past the last shores. They are
boarding the surf of the frail waters.*

*The resentful hope is confused. It is melting before I enter the
quiet Inn with shallow doors and drawn curtains where
blind alleys lead to forever quarters.*

*Let's not gaze past the sodden grounds in this forsaken land.
We might recognize a future barren abode unfolding
before us sitting quietly, just waiting...*

*As I myself get near the bitter crisp weather and ice-crystals
of eternal winter, I will proceed with extreme caution.
I will not betray the dead. I won't dance on their tomb!*

June 01, 2012.

DEBRIS

*I hide in the cuticle of my debris so that you can't see me crying
in the empty darkness that becomes untied at the
knife-edge of the pale night.*

*The scar resulting from your departure bites into my anguished soul.
The laughter fades before ancient music that now sounds as old
bells in a godforsaken barrack.*

**Now that I am alone, even lighting in its infancy troubles me. It sets
free sobs in the years of my emaciated love, as well as in solitary
captive nights where I howl in the moss so you can't hear my cry.**

**I reside in springs with storms, irises and essential gales that transport
mud of disheveled graves and obscure shades sweating before
they reach their destination.**

**In the winter, I dwell in the often forgotten realms east of the bosom
of my gaunt sleep that stays hidden in the fertile depths of the soil.**

**At the coal face of winter, you left your image in the debris of my liquid
soul where I am a partner of the underground water: an essential
element for my survival.**

**I am as a tuber which plunges deep into the fecund garden of the
earth and tumescent mud and unfinished shadows arriving
to its Cimmerian fate!**

November 28, 1997.

INDELIBLE

Gardens of images full of absent moons with sentiment,
and unaligned dark shadows are accosting me.

The arrangement of your body takes the breath away
of stars- spurting dances on cedar's indelible
shadows that enthrall all senses.

Isthmuses of white foam are igniting the ineffaceable
collapse over dawns of stone decanting over
the earth's tallow.

The hay wagon's encore is taking place over the prism
and border of the indelible, as my heart throbs and
endures forever over your shadow.

Yes, it's you and your face that is profoundly ingrained
in my outpost, before it limps onto the perch of
my indelible history that mesmerizes me.

March 29, 2005.

BEYOND OUR SORROWS

The seeds of mourning are drifting beyond the paths
and winds, walking past our assaulting sorrows
and the vines of our grieving disappointments.

The branches, twigs and leaves of many songs are
dispersing themselves amid the drunken sea of
our wounds. They are marching onward
to ameliorate our pain.

We're drowning in forests of hurt and anguish, but
these trivial aches don't dissuade us from battling
to overcome and triumph over these vicissitudes
along our darken trail.

Afar from the epicenter of our sullen choir, spring
is blossoming in cathedrals of light over the flesh
of the grazing lands being tended past the
hollow walls of our heart.

The shadows of winter are fleeing... unleashing hand
blown tears. They are attempting to crochet hope
past the invading breast of rain and storm beyond
the sorrows on our windowsill.

The lines between the sodden brooks and the fields of
glory are divided only by the moss that stands alone,
as though groping for faith and a desire for elusive
dreams beyond our sorrows.

Let's turn the tide!

Let's wrap our hurt in streams of dawns and births of
sanguine rainbows raided of gloom and despair.
August 22, 1989.

A RIPPLE IN THE LAND OF WATER

A ripple in the water leaves no handprint,
nor whispers of its sacred trail.

No mulch for eagles or smell nestling to engage the curious
man that is left.

The fearless frontiers are being crossed by water without
passing under imagined bridges churning in the
slopes of running rivers.

Our pilgrimage began over the speeding ripples crawling on
the passive waters staring at eternity and
a one-eyed river.

Ledges of clouds and swells of dreams are hanging in between
the whispers and wrinkles on this land water
hiding in silent bays.

Drunken ashes are falling in our awakened soliloquies, as we
walk on the edges of the rise and fall of Earth's dawn
where we are alive on its infinite undulations!

Whew. Let's catch our breath, before we become water
logged, before the sunlight and the silver
moon visit our trail.

November 24, 2018.

OUT OF AN INTIMATE FOG

Behind our narrative, we are being reduced to false
aged dispatches that exist only in the expansive
shores of a borrowed imagination.

We are emerging from storms that washed away
the sand from our clock, the oxygen from our
air and the light from our shadow.

November 28, 2013.

ON OUR MAIDEN VOYAGE

I am not here to dismember the molecules that bind us,
nor the shells of skeletons that wear enchanted
maternal whispers.
The stirring pain as well as the counting of heartbeats
clash aimlessly inside my small chest
looking for a compass.

I am here, in my inaugural crossing, in quest for my
salvation from the dreams that haunt me.
The shrill of an arsenal of deafening sounds resembles
tin-cans and marbles riding parallel to the slopes of
the dirt confronting my un-splintered lining.

On this passage, past the torrent of mist and the
chiaroscuro of the empty night, I hobble under
the quiet shadows.
The hollow trees wail their ancient voices at me, as the
images of fading moons rhapsody in my
waking fresh eyes and ears.

In this jaunt, the storms are nothing more than impending.
My heart is young. The images don't venture past
the naked light and the voice of the dawn staring
over my shoulder still smiles over the unoccupied
empty graves and muted rain.

May 31, 1966 – May 31, 1970 – June 01, 1982.

BLINDING DUST

On the path that appears... and disappears, dust flies
away with strangers, as the echoes of the disobedient
crossing are framed in our future.

In a single sound, a splash of images is seen conversing
with reissued constructed granite silence resting
inside jars of dust and ashes.

Dust is greeting us. A sudden earthquake is making the
shadow dance along with a posthumous flood parked
outside the dock of the gritty encrusted night.

Brushstrokes of pastel and chalk are posing before the
canvass perched on illusions... as a collection of
metaphors and paradoxes dreamt by my hand.

My virginal cardio-furrows are being flattened, as the
darkened night and blind dust are dressed to kill.

On the ancient ceiling of the museum, in the firmament's
fresco, a permanent collection of reclusive
treasures are beckoning for company.

Don't wait for me!

July 14, 2014.

SILHOUETTES

*The hidden images of my destiny are drawing graffiti on my
subterranean walls, as the voices of time murmur within
the outline of their own shadow: the voice of time
is indeed rudderless.*

I am not yet committed to my epitaph!

August 12, 2017.

POSTCARDS FROM THE SHADOWS

Under fractured moonlight, amputated shadows arrive
toward my fractured skeleton.

Postcards appear as lonesome rose petals and captive
royal empress tree leaves soar in cathedrals of winds
that are able to bend birds' wings.

They announce that winter is approaching to cover the
natural spires of the Earth, as well as the veins in
the spine of our diminished forest of dreams.

These shadows approach at a predictable tempo. They
mimic the rhythms of the Earth at the edge of
shackled time chewed by the teeth of the
creaking years.

These postcards arrive with photographs of screams
captured as rusted weightless umbra that shadow
boxes with the spirit of my haunting dreams.

Postcards from the edge of shadows are impaling my
enduring light which is swaying in a hammock in
the middle of an anonymous waning dance.

New dispatches are landing near my heart where
I am in mourning for the times long gone.
They've disembarked on emerging lands
that I once inherited.

May 07, 2015.

INSURGENT

I am an insurgent...born out of complete inconformity with the
flow of a hurried disintegrating world; this world full
of controls, rules and regulations, strewn needles,
bottle caps, covered asphalt paths and prefabricated
sidewalks. This world of extortion and imposition!

As a mutineer, I will always merge with the wild serpentinous
orchids, amber as well as rainbow colored.
I merge as well with the wild grasses and dandelions which
climb toward the forever expanding concrete if only to be
ripped violently and hastily even by virtuous juveniles.

During my uprising, I have not grown my winter hide yet to
prepare me for organic and man-made glass fragments
which downpour piercing my skin while demanding
closed-eyes and a well strengthened rind.

I assure you I can live in this world but only as a Red-crowned
woodpecker kept out to preserve my outer and inner
skin feathers, withered but not hostage or caged.

The silent inherited sound is parched with hard brazen noise
that blasts against spherical barriers that only create
stammered ephemeral echoes that stun me.

It may be that I am being baptized by concrete, by the
rudeness and disdain of this evolving microcosm.

Am I even part of this world? Am I made out of golden
or prophetic red clay?

June 01, 1969.

The Vigil for Freedom

*I wear the morning sunrise on my shoulders parallel to
the baked dust and the dreams scooped by time.*

*I'm bereft of transcendence, immersed by braided fires
looking to cross past the austere cotton and
my branded flesh.*

*My ancestral lands are empty, gashed by disengaged
auctioneers looking past what they see.*

*Our anatomy is painted in bank notes with promises of
blood, all embraced with greed stones burning white...
kindled by avarice.*

*For now, only the naked night is my friend and companion.
It gives respite to my weary trembling bones consumed
by the sun.*

*The flame of my soul can't be doused, as it marks time
within the furrows of my flesh.*

*My tears taunt the love and mercy of an unknown god whom
I'm calling from his vacation. Maybe his eyesight is wavering.*

Is slavery or god eternal?

*Let freedom reign within my mutilated molecules and the
shadows of my prayer.*

Am I betrothed to this land, my slave master or god?

February 18, 1975.

REQUIEM FOR OUR LAND

*Unimpeded, we encapsulate the previously visited dragons
on our tour crossing the wounded Earth.*

*Elliptically, we take flight clinging with hope to arrive before this
land's flame rendezvous with the dark hours at
the edgeless universe.*

*Turn right pass the scribbled lines on the overstretched Earth wistfully
sequestering clarion days, before its bewildering fate.*

*The silt and the echo of the Earth are barely living in the abstract
water's pure identity, before we slurp its polluted liquid content.*

*The sky is imbued with sunsets that are on warfare with the darkness
and destruction that is attempting to dirty our only vessel: the globe.*

*The powerful shoulders of the Earth are being shattered. They
are quietly trembling from its rendered trauma.*

*The dreams of our planet are becoming vacant and void of whispering
winds. They are entombed under unrecognizable weeping shores.*

*The Earth's light is being flooded under shapeless whirlpools of murky
ferreted poisons. The permanence of the Earth is in question.*

*The air and matter is brooding from its altered destiny, as it is being
bathed with torrents of souring streams capturing its molecules in venom.*

*The hymns to the birds and flowers of our land are falling in deep ponds full of
soundless... infinite whimpering silent wails...*

The murmur of death is approaching. The requiem for the Earth has begun!

April 22, 1980.
31

GRANDMA DO YOU STILL REMEMBER MY FACE?

As I looked into your closed eyes, I recall asking you whether you could still see my face as well as remember my face from heaven.

Perfume of a volcano and its smouldering ornamental bending shadow forms an integrated lament immersed in decaying weather along with the smell and sound of your forgotten footsteps.

Grandma, you provided my interior identity with depth, as I was an outcast huddled behind my childhood and its voracious appetite for our family's memory archives.

We are all leaving on ships of light lit by infinity and the torched burning snow that warms my soul.

Encapsulated ripples in puddles are starving to pierce the overwhelmed shadows of my prayers as I ransack the heavens looking for you.

Dearest Grandma, are you hosting an open house of dreams beyond the gazing dust in the elusive profundity in a sea of Jasmines?

Are your petals of silence still breaking the calm by singing lullabies for bees and dragonflies?

Remote shipwrecks and lost lightning and rain follow me to mock my flowering dreams without your protection.

A vessel of glacial water is being shepherded toward clouds of cedars drinking the enslaved long delayed afternoons inside my impassive desecrated atoms.

Grandma, I continue to see your peaceful face. I still hear your hush roaring past my extinction, tufted in the furrows of this earthly wasteland with cedar roots in the clouds.

Dearest grandma, your memory lives in between the grasslands and the soaring sky where you reside in, and around my wilderness.

December 20, 2003 – December 20, 2013.

TALES OF FAR AWAY MOONS

Secular serenity engulfs me as I voyage through the filled craters
of the earth rummaging through alien Easter Islands.

Moss is growing and thriving under molten glass baked by echoes
of unmoored treasures wearing far flung flesh tossing it
to the winds to ride on air currents.

Rain is rocking my world braided in granite where eternal time travel
blankets me with its discharging flash from far away moons.

Where are we going anyway?

JUNE 01, 1983 – JUNE 01, 2016.

FROM INSIDE THE EARTH

*The soil lies about its origins as it mingles with the enduring rippling
hordes of wheel-in shadows, smoke and soot that cover
our looming solitude.*

*Only dry dust overflows our vessel after the fire, as the weeds grow
off the root's branches to populate and stand as the silent
witnesses to our being.*

*The sap is brimming, striking, as lightning singes our cursed dreams,
mauling them back to expansive recycled energy and
its launched creation.*

*Are we goading the stone beholding our future, as well as the gazing
clouds trickling in between the sky's planks on our latitude?*

June 30, 2012.

PAST THE SHADOWS

Squandered shadows, dressed by the gaze of the mulatto canyons, stride out as an array of Dalmatian bruised silent outlines. They are being escorted by lopped elegies shunned by blindness.

Guiltless light is being lauded by rendered grace as I breathe at the compass of the river's blur. The road is narrow as the dusk dreams, floats and flutters discovering the intangible.

Tribes of corpses are awakened, getting ready to visit the parade that is ushered beyond the husk of the night's horizon stumbling to emerge on another shore.

Our life's roots are being whittled by time. They are fading, walking a tightrope on their way past the luring despair and indulgent lament announcing their end.

Time-travel is being jarred in a circle's weathered secant as it hums a requiem for our discreet spirit that lives in an island of indolent lament, not arousing any mutterings.

Candles are dribbling its last beads of wax. Rake in the last shelved sighs and dreams. The midnight rain will be flooding our land... burying our history under forgotten Oaks.

Let's navigate past the condemned forests of unburied limbs, still palpitating – gazing at life as unwashed orphans twirling their eyes in the mist.

Don't let thieves walk out with our trapped years still longing to pretend to dismiss death as an extinct hill.

I trust in life, the world that remains, and in the shimmering light mountains laden with Peace.

November 02, 2018.

DREAMS AND RUMOURS

Staircases are unloading their squinting gazes of yesterday.
They leave no footprints beyond the verified distressed
eyelids and vertigo noticed in the clouds.

The executioner's sprawling confrontation with his soul abounds.
The litany and crowning reason for the living is to avoid
huddling with river sorrows imprints that are carved
into our torrents of permanent detachment.

Glittering clamors and lumps of clay, as well as pulsar beacons
of nightfall, tell me fragmented tales of orbiting horizons
that will end in the birth of a dream.

The heart bookmark stumbles out of the pages of the book of
fables containing our invisible chimeras with wings, taking
us to the edge of contemplative waves in the heavens.

The questions proliferate as the tender reeling shades accost
us on our way to enduring the linking of limbs with those
who by now have left on barges that sailed into
consecrated unknown river ports.

The night, still ablaze with arrested images, contorts the scattered
bungled landscape as a response to a query, full of innuendo
and abstract dreams... seared in faulty intuition
and able reminiscence.

Chimeras never have a beginning, middle and discernable end.
They are the birth and death of life itself reared by flawless
proud eternal time!

May 31, 2002.

GALLOPING PAST TIME

I gallop past the shadow-less tentacles of time embracing the leather
flame rising to pierce the riverboat's hull floating on top of
sweet water ponds along with the birds of midnight.

The branches of my muted voyage have no memory, no recall of the
earth beating though kaleidoscopic glass harvesting the love
along its vigil for freedom amid wrinkled worn-out dreams.

Time was born under the naked light radiating from the heart of
melting clocks and hand painted rainbows cantering
on rivers of fire.

We stride past a world in quarrel with prolonged intoxicating farewells,
dismembered shadows as well as the remains of the cries grazing over
lost smuggled lands living at the edges of non-inventoried penumbras.

The slender seconds are accosting the nightingale's nests and the songs
flowing out of their throats, as I regurgitate shattered water
colored hunting queries.

The ripened enigmatic pre-ordained secretive byways are all sprouting
moss, as caged ashes are disguised as imperishable existence.

Musk vapors clothed in the radiant dawn of darkness are now visible.

Warp time is melting into the universe's paradox!!!

July 14, 2009.

IN PURSUIT

*I was born in the middle of a storm and had the entire mountain
range as my crib.*

*The flashes of lightning were messengers of my destiny. The sky's veil
clothed my humble haste to escape my ephemeral earthly harbor.*

*I was born as an heir of images, thoughts and fleeting premonitions
so I can share the bygone messages that were imparted through
the pursuit of dreams lost in the forest of silence
that ripped my soul.*

*Though my stay in my dwelling was brief, its incline hastened the self
enrichment and expansion of my dictionary and album of memories.*

*Now as the incline of my spine accelerates, I thank the years that
I walked on this wonderful and painful blue dwelling.*

*Under purple urban skies as well as golden fleecing moons, I was
a natural at meeting passions head on. They guided me through
jungles of reluctant origins as well as skyscrapers
of mythical distinction.*

*I am ready to reap the compensation for having survived in many
pieces. I guess it's in preparation to separate myself from
my corporeal bones.*

I am shipwrecked.

I am coming to lean on the armature of the Pyrenees.

May 31, 1967 – October 31, 2014

SOLITUDE

In the faraway farmlands of my solitude,
its emptiness still gazes at me
antagonistically.

At moments of despair, it bathes me in its waters.
My soul breaks out of this insular room
of fire through its key hole.

My life, tinged with kaleidoscopic muted colors, is blinded to
the black and white images, for they are always segregated.
Arbitrary ancient baritone songs are now
subdued and muted.

I can't hear them anymore unless there is someone to spoon
feed me before the notes dwindle from pristine kindling
to transubstantiated scarce ash.

Solitude never walks... it crawls inside our lobes, between my
temples and the ebbing pyre in our heart.

Solitude is never alone. It always accompanies the many,
for it needs them to adhere to like moss to stone.

Loneliness never separates itself from purgatory's penumbra
and its wilderness.

November 11, 1997.

I WON'T DANCE ON YOUR TOMB

*The rich dark baseboards on my porch are the same as in a revolving
door, evidence for those who believe in the elaborate tradition
of the origins of re-incarnation.*

*I don't wish to hear the chants with apostolic fervor that call us to
loath the vanished and hold them in contempt, for they are
still troubadours in life.*

*Soon I might be one of the wretched having intercourse with the gods
of the fallen, speaking in lost languages in sorely missed
sunken swamp islands.*

*Beyond the smoking rivers of mist, the birds sip the top of the foam
swimming by past the last shores. They are boarding the surf
of the frail waters.*

*The resentful hope is confused. It is melting before I enter the quiet
Inn with shallow doors and drawn curtains where blind alleys
lead to forever quarters.*

*Let's not gaze past the sodden grounds in this forsaken land. We might
recognize a future barren abode unfolding before us sitting
quietly, just waiting...*

*As I myself get near the bitter crisp weather and ice-crystals of
eternal winter, I will proceed with extreme caution.*

I will not betray the dead. I won't dance on their tomb!

June 01, 2012.

I AM GROWING ACQUAINTED WITH...

*I'm becoming familiar with this Earth as
I attempt to outpace the burning fire,
not restrained to the caged clouds
and the precincts of the moon.*

*I kneel before the scattering bark of the
moon plunging within the margins of
my stare as well as bound to the
boundaries of my harvested
remembrances.*

*The menacing shadow of the rain is
washing the willow branches in
preparation for the finches' visit
at the frontier of my
known memory.*

*I am growing acquainted with forlorn
hearts conversing with lingering
spirits living on idle islands of
despair waiting... for
the turning tide.*

July 27, 2018.

42

I HIDE

I hide and live in the solitary shores of your
naked eyelids from where no shadows
can clothe me or the compulsive fog
of my passion blind me.

I bury myself inside the cells of your flesh
so you will not notice me.

I walk along immersed with the dust
and dirt that accompanies your feet
as you walk away from the outline
of my heart.

I hide in a glacial intemperie behind
the silhouette of a purple snowflake
made out of glass.

May 30, 1992 -May 26, 2014.

AQUARELLE

My palm solemnly dips into the aquarelle which depicts
my face covered in winter dust and wearing
a crown made of icicles.

It thaws before your gaze. It smiles as it dresses in
the harbors of your heart and unpacks the invasive
raw quiet desolation of the cold.

I am only protected from the upcoming winter
storm by the canvas' borders which ride
on cirrus fermented rails!

June 20, 1985.

YOUR WINTER BONES ARE DRYING

Upon visiting my mother's gravesite on the 25TH anniversary of her departure.

*Your bones are pillars, vanishing sentinels of branches of history,
of the sagging, pruned hours… sleepless bones that roar
past the pendulum that govern us.*

*We are trudging past the blooming moon and the blows of the
driven rain aiming to wash away the history from your
bones in mid-decomposition.*

*The nightfall is crouching past the un-furnaced floor of your scowling
planks bending to let in the hydrangea's roots in order to
provide oxygen to your drying bones.*

*Inside your collapsing abode, a sea of air is spinning, trimming lost
generations, passing time and decay. They are overwhelming
my consequential and sequential history.*

*Your darkened splintered flames are not departing; they are breaking
the rhythms of my lifecycle. Don't be afraid to dance and
hitchhike away from this flesh-less terrain…*

*Your bones are returning to dust, as they are waking up to coax the
drums' skin syncopated beat. My heart is thumping parallel to
the meridian situated next to my breathing soul.*

*I have faith in my journey. It continues… our spirits are bait for
peace amid the rivers of our dreams in this leftover
land and time.*

The night train is still running...Call my name. I still hear you!

September 22, 2018.

I AM AT THE CONFLUENCE

I am at the confluence of ambling transmuted
magic shadows and an invented garden that
instead of hanging lilies, irises and roses;
they have dangling letters on
its paper branches.

The ripples of currents row its bouquet
toward me, to intoxicate my senses
long enough so I can pluck these
letters and mold them into
this dispatch.

Abandoned ripples of perfume bask in the
midst of sunlight just before accusatory
darkness stumbles and scatters my
words in every direction.

I am at the junction where the missing years
are lost in beseeching conversations that
are masquerading as a philosophical
conjunction with the self.

The association and struggle that threatens
the craving for love meet the scheme that
the chambers of our heart are in need of
for at least some fragmentary reality.

Our solitary structures are abdicating to rudderless
winds that will mock our wisdom for passion by
appealing to drunken gods that have never
hesitated to throw us into an endless
conflagration, that burns angels at
the crossroads of our grammar.

October 01, 2015.

HARKENING THE CALL

Soon we will enter misbegotten harbors,
desolate shores & inverted dreams.

We've graced ecliptic romantic earthly
habitats for what seems like a few days.

Though the journey was not long it had to end.
So the fondest of farewells dear earth!

Homeland of cleansing pain, you served
me well dearest mother and spirit.

Your love kept me tethered to this universe.

Mother earth, you were the vehicle that
transported me through endless time.

So finally, farewell flickering dusks, rain, half-moon
kettles and dormant skies. Farewell...

Greetings! Welcome dearest eternity.

Hello Buddha. We may now bivouac for all ages!

May 30, 1998.

PORTRAIT OF A DECANTED DREAM

Simmering

Boundless

Landscapes

Hummer

On its

Uninterrupted

Journey

Toward dusk

To gently

embrace

and sip

tomorrow's indomitable

sun rays.

Amidst   the chaos

of twinkling

clusters

of molecular

amalgamated shadows,

I gave birth

to myself!

May 31, 1995.

ABATED MURMURS

In the chiaroscuro world of life,
life is measured not by the weight of the breath,
but by the depth and pitch of the voice,
by the blend of the musical scale and the
metronomic constancy of our inner whispers.

Silence is not golden, but final!

Muted cries and desperate mirrors are
abated by the faint chirp of the heart.

Silence is not the quietude of the corporeal matter
but the incessant spectrum of rumble,
the murmuring tonality of an aboriginal flute recoiling
with every passage of wind tremulating to afar.

With the power of an imperceptible temblor
connecting one and all in a shared palpitation,
the collage of sounds dictate the scope of life,
not the quality, nor length of the pattern.

Life, as death,
is but a mere dislocation of time
between two parentheses!

21 February 1999.

WHISPERS

Withering whispers travel through bruised skies unmasking
pedestrian, confidential evidence scattered about
the true nature of our preconceptions.

Hollow whispers are launched across whirlpools of infinity,
invading veins of solitude in gardens with lighthouses
pointing to tourist islands of the heart.

Whispers travel where voices of birds read horoscopes
before a crowd attending country fairs.

They watch how our accompanying light plows beneath
the scaffolds to climb toward the gallows to marry
the Earth.

Whose whispers are escaping into the streams of unmade
rainbows and man-made springs that
sprout flowers?

Let's launch waves of withering whispers to drown all
the sighs from these prying people that are only
interested in being glanced by the
lighthouses' glares and shadows.

Islands of subconscious mindless intrusive enigmas
are part of subterranean fires that are guiding us
from below the robe of the sun?

A Shangri-la in mindless seas are being born as
a wedding place
for broken hearts and lost truths.

December 20, 2001 – August 12, 2005.

50

LET'S VANISH OBLIVION

Let oblivion be vanished. Let it fall into the depths of
unmarried crevasses and stormy seas that
fly on one wing.

Let remembrances become widowed by disobedient
waves that dawned in savage seas and empty
jungles made out of clay.

Cardio dispatches travel the purifying roads by
foot in my aging white dreams ...
only taking time to sojourn with moss cells.

Remembrances have to swim so as not to sink
on turbulent seas until they find a
natural death in the quarry of my dreams.

I've tilled a thousand hours in cold waters only
to harvest gloomy tempests that wear
seaweed for withered skin.

Let's put an end to blasphemous recollections that
are seeking sinister shelters inside
my painted veins.

I think I'll throw your recuerdo to a pyre where
only broken hearts and cadaverous sparrows
fuel the fire.

Let me walk away naked from the howls of my
orphan spirit.
Let oblivion forever dematerialize from my soul!

July 03, 1990 – July 03, 1996

TRANSITION

My testament's pages quiver as falling sycamore
leaves uncertain of their destiny and meaning.

They wrap around the veneer that intersect in the
dimming lines and my trembling wincing hand.

An earthquake is born.

The dimming light hushes as it converges with
the thinning air.

It is time for the lonely shadows to hold hands as
two nudes discovering the spilling night.

I guess the moon tides will have the final say and
translate the words that play with my heart.

Does it really matter?

As time rocks, I'll be my ancestor's neighbor soon.

I am wounded and I snarl as I attempt
to climb out of this riptide.

Is this a designated diminished bad dream?

What nerve and irreverence.

But I am not fraying...

May 31, 1972 – November 28, 2015.

ODE TO THE DARK SHADOWS

I sing to the dark shadows for those rescued from murky
rivers of gloom, the same that strolled through forests
of night to speak with the dead over meadows of silence
and proud seeds of nothingness.

I sing equally to the secret lakes filled from puddles of
mournful dark waters that stroll over fields of
granite, naked irises, lilies and hydrangeas.

I intone notes that accompany the lost dawns of steel,
whose advent of daybreak enlightens and spreads as
petals and ballads travelling on the back of
stray groaning winds.

As the Goldfinch's song scatters dawns of primitive hope
and brio, I sing to the rain to counter dark
purple auroras and veils of stone.

I want to sing to the brunette shadows that sow comfort on
homes of rubble, seedbeds of subdued extinguished seas,
caves of bodies in violent silence wailing forever resting on
tombs deprived of any calming wind and consoling music.

I rest on tombs deprived of threatening winds and
mysterious consoling music.

I sing an Ode to the dark shadows!

July 14, 2011 – July 14, 2015.

53

www.ingramcontent.com/pod-product-compliance
Lightning Source LLC
Chambersburg PA
CBHW080841250626
47161CB00009B/3152